Thomas Jefferson

Heroes of the American Revolution

★

Don McLeese

Rourke
Publishing LLC
Vero Beach, Florida 32964

www.rourkepublishing.com

PHOTO CREDITS: Cover Portrait, Pages 5, 10, 13, 14, 17, 24, 25, 27, 28, from the Library of Congress; Cover Scene, Page 6 ©Getty Images; Pages 9, 19, 29 ©North Wind Picture Archives; Title page, Pages 20, 23 ©PhotoDisc., Inc.

Title page: *Thomas Jefferson on Mount Rushmore*

Editor: Frank Sloan

Cover and page design by Nicola Stratford

Library of Congress Cataloging-in-Publication Data

McLeese, Don.
  Thomas Jefferson / Don McLeese.
    p. cm. -- (Heroes of the American Revolution)
  Includes bibliographical references and index.
  ISBN 1-59515-217-2 (hardcover)
  1. Jefferson, Thomas, 1743-1826--Juvenile literature. 2. Presidents--United States--Biography--Juvenile literature. I. Title. II. Series: McLeese, Don. Heroes of the American Revolution.
  E332.79.M38 2004
  973.4'6'092--dc22

                         2004007607

Printed in the USA

LB/LB

Table of Contents

An American Leader 4

Early Years 7

Moving to Tuckahoe 8

School Days .11

Away from Home 12

His Father's Death 15

Becoming a Lawyer 16

A Voice for Freedom 18

Marrying Martha 21

The Continental Congress 22

Words to Live By 25

Home to Virginia 26

A Great American 28

Time Line 30

Glossary 31

Index 32

Further Reading/Websites to Visit 32

An American Leader

Thomas Jefferson was a great thinker and writer who became one of the best presidents of the United States. During the Revolutionary War period, he was one of the most famous and important American leaders. America no longer wanted to be ruled by England. Americans wanted to elect their own leaders.

In 1776, America declared its freedom from England by issuing the Declaration of **Independence**. Thomas Jefferson wrote the Declaration, with its famous words that "All men are created equal."

Jefferson believed in **democracy**, where voting gives Americans an equal voice in their government. After the Declaration of Independence that Jefferson wrote, America won its war with England and earned the freedom to become its own country: the United States of America.

Benjamin Franklin, John Adams, and Thomas Jefferson (standing) read a draft of the Declaration of Independence.

A MAP of
the most INHABITED part of
VIRGINIA
containing the whole PROVINCE of
MARYLAND
with Part of
PENSILVANIA, NEW JERSEY and NORTH CAROLINA
Drawn by
Joshua Fry & Peter Jefferson
in 1751.

the Right Honourable, George Dunk Earl of Halifax First Lord Comn
to the Rest of the Right Honourable and Honourable Commissioners, for TRADE and PLAS
This Map is most humbly Inscribed to their Lordships,
By their Lordships
Most Obedient & most devoted humble Serv.t Thos. Jef

A picture of a map drawn by Peter Jefferson and Joshua Fry

Early Years

★

Thomas Jefferson was born on April 13, 1743 in Virginia. His family was very wealthy and lived on a large, 2,500-acre (1,012-hectare) farm that they called Shadwell.

His father, Peter Jefferson, was one of the most **respected** men in the area. Thomas's mother, Jane Randolph Jefferson, was from one of the oldest families in Virginia. Thomas's mother loved to write, and her son would share that love. He was the third child in his family, with six sisters and a brother.

CALENDAR CHANGE

Thomas was born nine years before the calendar changed to the one we use now. His birth date on the calendar used then was April 2. The new calendar changed that date to April 13.

〜

Moving to Tuckahoe

★

When Thomas was three years old, he and his family left Shadwell and moved to another farm called Tuckahoe. It was 50 miles (80 km) away and took three days for the Jeffersons to reach by horses and carts. Tuckahoe was owned by William Randolph, who was Peter's friend and Jane's cousin. After William died, the Jeffersons moved from their house to his nicer one to take care of it.

Thomas had little memory of those early years in Shadwell. Instead, he remembered Tuckahoe as his boyhood home. There was a one-room country schoolhouse behind the Tuckahoe house, and it was here that Thomas first learned to read and write.

ONE~ROOM SCHOOLHOUSE

Today, students are taught in different rooms for different grades, depending on the age of the student. Back then, children of all different ages were taught in one room.

~

Thomas Jefferson attended school at the Tuckahoe Schoolhouse.

A colonial schoolteacher walks with her many students.

School Days

★

Thomas was five years old when he first went to the school. The private teacher hired by his father taught Thomas arithmetic as well as reading and writing. In those days, it was important to write very clearly, because there weren't any computers to type on. Thomas became very good at **penmanship**, and was known as a very smart student.

Away from Home

★

When Thomas was nine, his family moved back to Shadwell. There wasn't a good school there, and Thomas's father thought his son needed to learn. So the family sent Thomas to live at a nearby school in Dover Creek. Thomas missed being home, but he learned a lot at school. He read a lot of the most famous books, called **classics**.

Thomas lived during the school year for five years at Dover Creek. During the summer, he would return to Shadwell and help on the farm.

Learning was difficult for many colonial children.

A scene of Virginia countryside similar to the land where Jefferson grew up

His Father's Death

★

In 1757, when Thomas was 14 years old, his father died. Peter Jefferson was only 49 years old, but people didn't live as long back then. As the oldest son, Thomas became head of the family. He had to return home to take care of Shadwell. He still went to school, though, because he was very smart and wanted to do more with his life than run the farm.

Becoming a Lawyer

★

When Thomas was 16, he went to the College of William and Mary in Williamsburg. Only the very smartest students went to college in those days, and many of them went there when they were young, as Thomas did. During his years at college, Thomas learned a lot more about science, mathematics, and religion.

He decided while he was there that he wanted to be a lawyer, so he started studying law as well. He finished college after two years in 1762 and then went to work at a lawyer's office. He still studied law. In 1767, Thomas Jefferson became a lawyer. He was known as a very good one.

PASSING THE BAR

In order to become a lawyer, then or now, you need to pass a test called the "bar exam." This is called "passing the bar," which is what Thomas did in 1767.

~

A period drawing of the College of William and Mary

A Voice for Freedom

★

In 1769, voters elected Thomas Jefferson to the House of **Burgesses**, which helped England govern the colony of Virginia. Thomas was not a great speaker, but he became known in the House as a great writer. He took the side of those who felt that America should be free from Britain, that it should become its own country.

A portrait of Thomas Jefferson

A modern photograph of Monticello, Jefferson's home

Marrying Martha

★

In 1771, Thomas Jefferson fell in love with a woman named Martha Wayles Skelton. She was a widow. Her father was a lawyer, just like Thomas. She loved music, and so did Thomas.

Thomas Jefferson married Martha on New Year's Day, January 1, 1772. Jefferson had already begun building the house where he wanted to live. He called it Monticello.

MONTICELLO

In Italian, "Monticello" means "little mountain." Thomas built his mansion on a hill in Shadwell, the family farm of his boyhood. Monticello remains very famous, and many people visit the home every year.

~

The Continental Congress

★

In 1775, Virginia made Thomas one of its members of the Second **Continental** Congress. This Congress had many members who wanted America to become its own country. In the spring of 1776, the Continental Congress appointed a committee to write the Declaration of Independence. Jefferson was asked to write it. He spent 17 days writing and rewriting the paper that would declare America's independence from England.

INDEPENDENCE DAY

The Second Continental Congress voted to approve the Declaration of Independence on July 4, 1776. Ever since, the United States has celebrated the Fourth of July as our nation's birthday, or "Independence Day."

~

Independence Hall in Philadelphia, where the Declaration of Independence was signed

Signing the Declaration of Independence

Words to Live By

★

In the Declaration of Independence, Jefferson wrote that "all men are created equal" and have the rights to "life, liberty and the **pursuit** of happiness." When a government becomes "destructive of these ends, it is the right of the people to alter or to **abolish** it, and to **institute** a new government..."

In other words, if the British government wouldn't give Americans their rights, it was the right of America to change that government and become its own country. A government that depends on the votes of the people to elect a leader is called a democracy.

Signers of the Declaration of Independence leave Independence Hall.

THE REBELS OF '76. OR, THE FIRST ANNOUNCEMENT OF
THE GREAT DECLARATION.

Home to Virginia

★

Jefferson didn't become a soldier or a general to fight the Revolutionary War. He thought he could serve his country better by becoming part of the government of Virginia. He returned to Virginia in September, 1776, and helped make laws as a member of the House of Delegates. He was elected governor in 1779 and 1780.

In 1782, his wife died, which made Jefferson very unhappy. When Virginia elected Thomas Jefferson to Congress in 1783, he hoped this would help him get over his sadness.

A portrait of Thomas Jefferson around the time of his wife's death

A Great American

★

Thomas Jefferson continued to serve his country. He became vice president to John Adams, the second president of the United States, after finishing second to Adams in the election of 1796. In 1801, Thomas Jefferson was elected president. He served from 1801-1809, and is remembered as one of the best and most famous presidents in this country's history. During his presidency, his Louisiana Purchase of land from France almost doubled the size of the new country.

But even if Jefferson had never become president, he would be remembered as an American hero for writing the Declaration of Independence. It is fitting that he died at Monticello on July 4, 1826, exactly 50 years to the day after the Declaration was approved.

John Adams, the second president of the United States

Jefferson arrives for his inauguration as president.

Time Line

1743 ★ Thomas Jefferson is born.

1757 ★ Jefferson's father dies.

1762 ★ Jefferson finishes college after two years.

1767 ★ Jefferson passes the bar exam and becomes a lawyer.

1769 ★ Jefferson is elected to the House of Burgesses.

1772 ★ Jefferson marries Martha Wayles Skelton.

1775 ★ Jefferson is made a member of the Second Continental Congress.

1776 ★ Jefferson writes the Declaration of Independence.

1779~80 ★ Jefferson is elected governor of Virginia.

1782 ★ Jefferson's wife dies.

1783 ★ Jefferson is elected to Congress.

1796 ★ Jefferson finishes second to Adams in presidential election.

1801~09 ★ Jefferson serves as president.

1826 ★ Jefferson dies.

Glossary

abolish (a BOL ish) — to end or to make illegal

burgesses (BUR jes ez) — representatives elected to help make laws in England (and in America before it became its own country)

classics (KLAS ikz) — the most important books (or music or other works of art) in history

continental (KONT un ENT ul) — on or of the continent

democracy (di MOK ruh see) — government by the people, who vote to elect their leaders

independence (IN duh PEN dunts) — freedom from another government

institute (IN stuh TOOT) — to set up or put in place

penmanship (PEN mun ship) — handwriting

pursuit (per SOOT) — the act of going after something, trying to get something

respected (rih SPEKT ud) — admired, thought to be a very good person

Index

Adams, John   28

College of William and Mary   16

Delcaration of Independence   4, 17

Dover Creek   12

House of Burgesses   18

Louisiana Purchase   28

Monticello   21, 28

Revolutionary War   26

Second Continental Congress   22

Skelton, Martha Wayles   21

Shadwell   7, 8, 12, 15

Tuckahoe   8

Virginia   7, 18, 22, 26

Williamsburg   16

Further Reading

Emerson, Julie. *Thomas Jefferson.* Capstone Press, 2003

Nardo, Don. *Thomas Jefferson.* Scholastic Library Publishing, 2003

Pingry, Patricia A. *The Story of Thomas Jefferson.* Ideals Publications, 2003

Websites to Visit

etext.lib.virginia.edu/jefferson/
www.whitehouse.gov/history/presidents/tj3.html
www.loc.gov/exhibits/jefferson/

About the Author

Don McLeese is an award-winning journalist whose work has appeared in many newspapers and magazines. He earned his M.A. degree in English from the University of Chicago, taught feature writing at the University of Texas and has frequently contributed to the World Book Encyclopedia. He lives with his wife and two daughters in West Des Moines, Iowa.